When Jungle Jim Comes To Visit Fred The Snake

Written by

Peter B. Cotton

illustrated by

Bonnie Lemaire

Peter Cotton
Feb 2015

www.petercottontales.com

THE FIG & THE VINE
PUBLISHING, LLC

This Book Belongs To:

This book is dedicated to my wonderful family, and all friends of Fred.

Remember Fred, the friendly snake,
who lost his head half by mistake,
when squished in two by ambulance wheels?
Can you imagine how that feels?

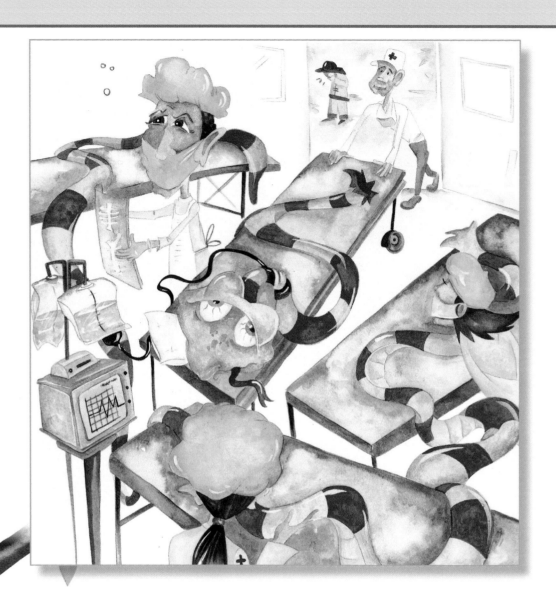

But the Doctor with some thread,
(that Jim found in a Rhino's bed),
saved the day by carefully sewing
Fred-Fred's coming to his going.

To learn about it you should look,
at the very first Fred book.

Check the second book as well, where we illustrate and tell, how Fred and I (both so cool), went together to my school. The kids were rather scared at first, thinking Fred might bite, or worse.

But Fred made lots of friends
when he used his slinky bends
to give us useful things at school—
a big slide for the swimming pool,

a jump rope, then a soccer goal,
and a bendy fishing pole.
Together we had fun each day,
at school, at home, and out at play.

But I saw Fred in tears one night,
sniffling as he tried to write,
a little note to Jungle Jim,
to say that he was missing him.
Being a solitary snake, the "only",
made him sometimes rather lonely.
Surely Jim could make amends,
perhaps visit with some jungle friends?

Jim was used to being alone,
but recognizing Fred's sad tone,
decided he and friends should come,
to see Fred's newly chosen home.
Jim cranked up his jungle bike,
collected things that Fred might like,
and stacked them on two trolleys
which he found rusting, in a ditch.

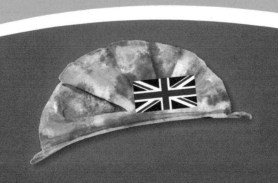

Then Jim decided who to take.
He chose a lovely lady snake,
and some parrot birds to fly,
to check the best route from the sky...
A mongoose and a pair of sloth,
Jim agreed to take them both,
a giraffe who had schooled with Fred,
came to watch the road ahead,
and then, bringing up the rear,
two monkeys and a baby deer.

A tiger really wanted in,
but Jim was nervous taking him.
Tigers have a lot of bounce
and a tendency to pounce!
Jim didn't want to be a snack
while he cruised the jungle track.
The trolleys were all loaded,
so Jim announced, "It's time to go!"

"We'll take this track I've used before,
it takes us to the ocean shore.
I hope we'll find the nice old ship
that brought me here on my first trip."
Jim pedaled bravely over bumps,
avoiding when he could, the stumps,
and when he landed in a bush,
an elephant was there to push.

"There it is," Jim cried, "That boat —
it should keep us all afloat."
He quickly drove up on the deck,
and tied things down so's not to wreck.

18

19

Soon enough they all
set sail, taking directions
from a whale.
The ocean proved
a little rough,
but Jim and friends
were brave enough.

21

It wasn't many days before
they landed on the distant shore.
A wooden sign there in the sand read
"Welcome to this Special Land!
Surely nothing could be finer,
than to be in Carolina."
Where does Fred live? No need to guess,
Jim checked his jungle GPS,
and got directions to the street,
where he knew they all would meet.

Fred and I just had to wait,
standing by our garden gate,
hoping that we soon would see
Jungle Jim's menagerie.
Then round the corner, way up high,
we saw a giraffe's head and eye.
We were bursting with delight
as the travelers came in sight!

Jim halted, panting, in our yard
(the pedaling was awfully hard).
The animals woke up with a
start and tumbled from the jungle cart.

Mama, with a happy face, said
"You are welcome to this place.
You must be hungry, so I've made
some burgers and pink lemonade.
And I took the time to bake
a great big yummy chocolate cake!"

"Tomorrow we will show you all
our little town and local mall.
Maybe we could go to school,
and cool down in the swimming pool.
But when you need to cross the road,
please don't forget your crossing code."
Fred remembers, and he wishes,
that no one else will get the squishes.

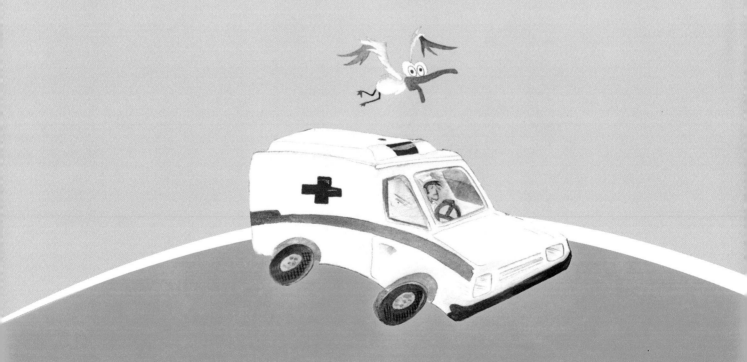

"Now I think it would be best
for all of you to get some rest.
You'll see our house is rather small,
and can't accommodate you all.
But a neighbor friend has lent his
very large exploring tent.

Jim can sling his hammock there,
and sloths can dangle anywhere.
You birds should gather
up some leaves and make your
nests beneath the eves."

The lady snake was lonely
so she knew exactly where to go.
She slithered slowly up to Fred,
"My name is Bernadette," she said.
"I bring greetings from your chums,
especially your Dad and Mum.
All jungle folks are pleased to hear
that you are happy living here."

Fred smiled shyly as he said,
"Please put your box beside my bed,
I am very pleased to share,
this little place beneath the stair.
You can tell me jungle news,
and I will do my best to try
to share what I have learned so far:
at school, at home, and in the car."

We checked that Jungle Jim was right.
His friends were settled for the night.
Judging by their smiles it seems,
that they are having happy dreams.
And snoring from the eves suggests
the birds were comfy in their nests.
They dream of happy times to come,
with Fred and me and my Mum.
So many things to see and do,
we are excited, aren't you?

To see what happens you should
look at the very next Fred book.
Join us when we will explore
Charleston, Dewees Isle and more.
Now it's time to douse the light,
tell Bernadette and Fred goodnight,
and to show how much you care,
bless them with a little prayer.

This is the third book about Fred the friendly Snake. The first, *When Fred The Snake Got Squished and Mended,* tells how he became Fred-Fred when crossing the road, but happily was mended by a clever doctor using special thread sent by Jungle Jim. In the second book, *When Fred The Snake Goes To School,* Fred was happy and popular because he could play games well and twist himself into useful things like a soccer goal and a water-slide. But he was lonely, and wrote to Jungle Jim asking him to come and visit. So now we read how Jim bravely journeys across the ocean to visit Fred, with other jungle friends, including a lady snake called Bernadette.

 **Dr. Peter Cotton** was born in Herefordshire, England, where his father was a country physician. He was educated at Cambridge University and at St. Thomas Hospital Medical School (London), and graduated as a doctor in 1963. He eventually became a Gastroenterologist, and ran a leading department at The Middlesex University Hospital in London, before moving to USA in 1986 to become Professor of Medicine at Duke University in North Carolina. In 1994, he moved again to set up the Digestive Disease Center at the Medical University of South Carolina in Charleston. He recently retired from clinical work but continues part-time in research and teaching. He has written many medical textbooks, almost 1,000 scientific papers, and recently published his memoirs entitled *The Tunnel at the End of the Light: My Endoscopic Journey in Six Decades.* (www.peterbcotton.com)

Peter Cotton first wrote about *Fred the Snake* for his then young children almost 40 years ago, but publication began only after he found a perfect illustrator partner, Bonnie Lemaire. (www.bonniella.com)

When Fred the Snake Got Squished and Mended was awarded the "Best Rhythmic Book" prize by a New York company "Story Time Jam—This Book Rocks" in 2013.

Learn more (including why Peter Cotton
was not named after a rabbit) at
www.petercottontales.com

43

CPSIA information can be obtained
at www.ICGtesting.com
Printed in the USA
LVIC01n1219081213
364096LV00002BA/2